A RAINBOW BALLOON

A Book of Concepts

written and photographed by

ANN LENSSEN

COBBLEHILL BOOKS
Dutton · New York

ACKNOWLEDGMENTS

I would like to express appreciation to the pilots and chase team of
Climb on a Rainbow Balloon Flights for sharing *Tickled Pink* with us.

Library of Congress Cataloging-in-Publication Data
Lenssen, Ann.   A rainbow balloon : a book of concepts /
written and photographed by Ann Lenssen.   p.   cm.
Summary: Introduces basic concepts such as rise and
fall and one and many while following "Tickled Pink,"
a rainbow colored hot-air balloon, on a flight.
ISBN 0-525-65093-8
1. Hot air balloons—Juvenile literature.
2. Ballooning—Juvenile literature.   [1. Hot air balloons.
2. Balloon ascensions.   3. English language—Synonyms
and antonyms.]   1. Title. TL638.L46   1992
629.133'22—dc20   91-31830   CIP   AC

Published in the United States by Cobblehill Books,
an affiliate of Dutton Children's Books,
a division of Penguin Books USA Inc.
375 Hudson Street, New York, New York 10014

Designed by Kathleen Westray
Printed in Hong Kong   First Edition

10   9   8   7   6   5   4   3   2   1

Dedicated to that spark of curiosity in children which inspires them to find out how things work.

Drifting overhead in a rainbow of colors, is a hot-air balloon named *Tickled Pink*. How does it stay up there? What makes the balloon come back down? Follow along and see.

top

The colored fabric part—the top—is called an envelope.

bottom

Passengers ride at the bottom in a strong, wicker basket.

inside

The inside of the envelope looks like
a stained-glass window . . .

outside

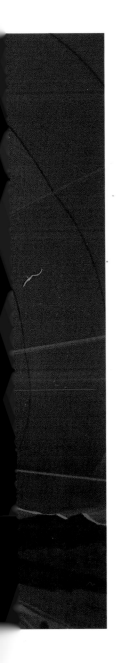

...and the outside, a giant beach ball.

push

With a big push, the heavy wicker basket
is unloaded at the launch site.

pull

To keep the balloon from rising too rapidly,
a crew member pulls on the crown line.

open

A large opening at the top of this balloon
is a parachute vent.

closed

The vent is closed with Velcro fasteners attached to a circular piece of fabric. A long rope inside leads from the vent to the basket. At the end of the flight the pilot pulls on the rope to open the vent and let out the air.

hot

Flames from the flight burner will make the air inside the balloon hot. This safety preflight test shows that all the equipment works properly.

cold

A powerful fan fills the envelope two-thirds of the way with cold air. Then heat may be added without damaging the fabric.

off

The flight burner is attached to the basket
and aimed at the top of the envelope. Except
for the preflight safety test, it remains off
until the pilot is ready to add heat.

on

Hoses lead from tanks of propane fuel to the burner. The pilot turns on the flight burner by opening the blast valve.

empty

With no air inside, the empty envelope
looks like a long silky scarf.

full

Air stretches out the envelope until it is full.

Because it is lighter than cold air,
hot air makes the balloon rise.

fall

After a landing, the parachute vent is opened.
With a rustle, the envelope falls to the ground.

noisy

The burning propane makes a noisy whooshing
sound while adding heat to lift the balloon.
The burner is used during a flight only when
the pilot wishes to add heat to the envelope.

quiet

In between blasts of burning propane, *Tickled Pink* drifts quietly, making no sound at all.

near

Standing near, *Tickled Pink* is taller than a six-story building.

far

But when far away, it is a pink
dot hanging in the sky.

low

Balloons fly low, just above the trees...

high

... or as high as 3,000 feet.

many

Often many balloons are launched together...

one

. . . or just one, all by itself.

light

Out in the sunlight, the balloon
casts a big shadow.

dark

Using the burner in the dark makes
the balloon glow like a lantern.

up

Tickled Pink rides the wind up above treetops.

down

To land, the pilot uses the burner less often. As the air cools, *Tickled Pink* comes down in a meadow.

Pilots look for landing sites with
no buildings and power lines.

Soft landings, *Tickled Pink!*